THE SHADE
OF DEATH

ROKK
THE WALKING
MOUNTAIN

With special thanks to James Noble

For Jed Thomas Burden

www.beastquest.co.uk

ORCHARD BOOKS
338 Euston Road, London NW1 3BH
Orchard Books Australia
Level 17/207 Kent St, Sydney, NSW 2000

A Paperback Original
First published in Great Britain in 2009

Beast Quest is a registered trademark of Working Partners Limited
Series created by Beast Quest Limited, London

Text © Working Partners Limited 2009
Cover and inside illustrations by Steve Sims © Orchard Books 2009

A CIP catalogue record for this book is available from
the British Library.

ISBN 978 1 40830 439 6

5 7 9 10 8 6 4

Printed and bound by CPI Group (UK) Ltd, Croydon, CR0 4YY

The paper and board used in this paperback are natural recyclable
products made from wood grown in sustainable forests. The
manufacturing processes conform to the environmental regulations
of the country of origin.

Orchard Books is a division of Hachette Children's Books,
an Hachette UK company

www.hachette.co.uk

ROKK
THE WALKING MOUNTAIN

BY ADAM BLADE

ORCHARD

THE ICE CASTLE
CRESCENT CAVE
FREGSHOR
GWILDORIAN PLAINS
THE RAINBOW JUNGLE

Gwildor

GWILDORIAN OCEAN

MLAND

FISHING
VILLAGE

*W*elcome to a new world...

Did you think you'd seen all the evil that existed? You're almost as foolish as Tom! He may have conquered Wizard Malvel, but fresh challenges await him. He must travel far and leave behind everything he knows and loves. Why? Because he has six Beasts to defeat in a kingdom he can't even call home.

Will his heart be in it? Or will Tom turn his back on this latest Quest? Little does he know, but he has close ties to the people here. And a new enemy determined to ruin him. Can you guess who that enemy is...?

Read on to see how your hero fares.

Velmal

PROLOGUE

"Home!" Briel gasped, as he reached
the peak of the North Mountain. The
town of Tion spilled out across the
valley below him.

He paused to catch his breath and
give his aching legs time to recover.
Stone huts with thatched roofs lined
the dusty brown roads linking the
North and South Mountains that
loomed over Tion.

It was market day. Briel knew
that traders from all over northern
Gwildor would be making their way
to Tion.

Behind him, he heard a chorus
of bleating. He glanced over his
shoulder at the herd of goats he'd
driven from the nearby town of
Kewas. It was Briel's job to make
sure that none of the animals
were lost during the trip across
the treacherous mountains.

He looked back at Tion. Memories of
his sister's cooking made his stomach
rumble. After a week of eating
nothing more than honey-cakes,
a freshly roasted chicken was just
what he needed.

"Why am I wasting time?" he
wondered. "Let's get home!"

As Briel strode forwards, he heard

a low, grating sound – like rock scraping across rock. He felt vibrations beneath his feet; he paused, head cocked, listening carefully.

Faint voices suddenly sounded from below: "Flee! Run away!"

Briel scrambled back to the top of the peak for a better view. Down in Tion, chaos had erupted – bolting horses threw their riders; mothers and fathers scooped up young children and fled; traders bundled up as many of their wares as they could carry. Everyone was running.

Briel narrowed his eyes, desperately trying to pick out his sister among the panicking crowds. Where was she? *Please let her be safe*, he thought.

A blur of movement on the far mountain suddenly caught his attention.

"Avalanche!" Briel gasped.

Dozens of boulders tumbled down the South Mountain, smashing into the ground and careering in every direction, gaining speed. They crashed into homes, sending wooden beams and stone flying. It was the most ferocious avalanche Briel had ever seen. Then, suddenly, the momentum of the rocks came to a halt, freezing them to the spot.

"It's almost as if they *decided* to stop," gasped Briel. He was dimly aware of the goats behind him, panicking and running in every direction.

Slowly at first, the rocks began to slide along the ground, smashing together, the impact sending jagged shards shooting into the air. The sound echoed through the valley.

The rocks formed a shape. Legs made of long stones straightened up and attached to a giant, flat slab.

A body.

Other rocks flexed either side of the body. Arms. As Briel watched, slack-mouthed, one last boulder slid into place on top. A head, with a curling crack for a mouth and two gaping chasms for eyes. One of the eyes shone a curious shade of green.

With an ear-splitting screech, the head turned as the terrifying creature surveyed the destruction of Tion. His right eye pulsed with a bright green light as he extended one of his arms, tearing up the last remaining tree by its roots, tossing it aside as easily as a twig. Briel realized his whole body was trembling as he watched the Beast's angry gaze travel around the town.

At least the townsfolk have escaped,
he thought. He could see them now,
running south-westwards. *Please let
my sister be among them.*

If he hurried, he could catch up with
them – and hopefully be reunited
with his sister. He clicked his tongue
at the terrified goats, who turned
to follow him. Briel decided he
would take the long route round to
the west of Tion. That was the best
way of keeping hidden from the
rock Beast who, even now, gave a
crooked smile at the flattened village.
Briel knew that if one of those huge
rock fists came down on him, he
would never survive…

CHAPTER ONE

A NEW VENTURE

"I wish I had arrows that replaced themselves," said Elenna. "That would be much easier."

Tom watched Elenna as she sat on the ground, whittling arrow shafts from pine twigs. The tip of her tongue poked out of her mouth as she frowned with concentration. Tom grinned, before turning to look out across the lush plains of Gwildor.

Tom had never heard of this
kingdom until the good wizard Aduro
had told him that six new Beasts
needed rescuing from the curse of
Velmal. Thinking about the wizard
and his evil magic made Tom reach
out a protective hand to his horse,
Storm. Nearby, Elenna's wolf Silver
sat on his haunches, keenly watching
his mistress work.

"Can I help?" Tom asked.

Elenna smiled up at him. "It took me years to learn how to whittle like this," she said, teasing. "You may be Avantia's Master of the Beasts, but it's best to leave this to me."

"My father is Master of the Beasts now," he reminded her. "I'm back to being Tom."

Pride flooded his chest as he recalled the Quest that had saved his father, Taladon, from being trapped as a ghost. Tom had needed to find all six pieces of the Amulet of Avantia that now hung around his neck.

Tom held up the Amulet. On one side, brilliant blue enamel gleamed in the centre. On the other was etched an intricate map of the kingdom of Gwildor, directing them on their travels. With each new Quest, the map guided Tom and Elenna to the location of the next Beast, and to a prize that would help him conquer each new foe. Against Krabb, Master of the Sea, he had used a magic pearl that allowed him to breathe underwater. Against Hawkite, arrow of the air, he'd found an enchanted ring that made him invisible when he stood still.

The prizes had been invaluable in his Quest so far. But they did not belong to him. They belonged to Freya, Gwildor's Mistress of the Beasts.

"What's wrong?" Elenna asked. "You're frowning."

"I was just thinking about Freya," he replied. "She was this kingdom's champion, and Velmal made her evil. She told me she doesn't want to be good again. I don't understand it."

Elenna placed her new arrows in her quiver, before flinging it over her shoulder. She stood up. "That's Velmal's dark magic talking. Once we complete this Quest, maybe Freya will become good again."

"I hope so," said Tom. "Gwildor is Avantia's twin kingdom. If it falls into darkness, then…" He couldn't bring himself to say it. The thought of evil spreading across the ocean to Avantia was too dreadful to think about.

"Tom!" said Elenna, pointing at the amulet in Tom's hand. It pulsed with a blue light.

Tom held it up. Elenna stood behind him, looking over his shoulder. The map showed two roads running side by side to a mountainous region in north Gwildor. At the end of the first path was a tiny image of a pair of gloves. At the end of the other was a pair of towering mountains. Beneath them was some swirly writing.

"Rokk," Elenna read aloud. "The next Beast's name."

"Yes, but where is he?" Tom mused. There was no picture of a Beast on the map.

Elenna shrugged. "Lurking in the mountains?" she suggested. "Maybe he has a cave up there? I wonder what kind of Beast he is?"

Tom checked Storm's saddle. "It doesn't matter," he told her. "We have to find the gloves first. We can worry about the Beast later."

Tom climbed into the saddle. "Ready?" he asked, offering Elenna a hand.

His friend pulled herself up behind him. "I'm always ready," she said, with a laugh. Tom felt her arms wrap around his waist as Storm set off at a trot.

Tom gripped the reins tightly, but felt a sudden twinge of pain in his right hand. Glancing down, he saw that the skin was still tinged green from Krabb's attack. Worse, the green poison had travelled further up his arm. Tom pulled on Storm's reins, bringing the stallion to a stop.

"What's wrong?" Elenna asked.

"I'm just tired from the last Quest," Tom said, telling Elenna a white lie. He didn't want her to worry. "Would you mind taking the reins?"

Elenna playfully poked him in the ribs as they swapped places. "Don't fall asleep back there," she teased. "You've got the map, after all!"

"I won't," Tom said, climbing into the saddle behind her. He tried to ignore the hollow feeling of dread in the pit of his stomach. The truth was, his hand was hurting so much that he'd had trouble keeping a tight grip on the reins.

As Storm cantered forwards, a question swirled around Tom's mind, refusing to go away. *What happens if I can't hold my sword anymore?* If Tom couldn't fight, the Beast Quest would be over.

CHAPTER TWO

THE DARK STORM

"Storm's struggling," said Elenna, as the path dipped treacherously and the stallion's hooves slipped. "The ground is too uneven."

Tom looked ahead. They had ridden hard and fast, and were now amongst the mountain ranges. The sky was a vivid blue and the snowy peaks dazzled with a brilliant white light. But the path was steep.

"You're right," Tom said, dismounting. "Let's get down and walk. Rokk could be hiding nearby. If we go slowly, we'll be able to spot any sudden movements."

Clutching Storm's reins in his uninjured hand, Tom led his stallion up a sloping rocky path. Silver scampered ahead of them, nose in the air. They soon found a rocky plateau that felt safe enough to stop for food. The sun was at its highest point, and the thin mountain air was so hot that Tom felt beads of sweat spring out on his temples.

"It's gorgeous here," Elenna breathed, standing at the edge of the plateau's edge. Far below, the valley sloped away from the mountains. The grass was deep green and bubbling springs twinkled in the

sunlight. "It's just odd that a land
so beautiful contains such...evil."

"The Beasts will be good again,"
Tom said. "Once we free them from
Velmal's magic."

"I didn't mean the Beasts," said Elenna, taking some bread and cheese out of Storm's saddlebag. "I meant Velmal and Freya."

"Freya can be saved. I'm sure of it," Tom said. He felt an ache in his heart. Why did he care so much about what happened to Freya? He'd already come across many people affected by evil magic on his Quests. Why was this woman any different from the others? "I'll free her from Velmal's magic, just like I will the Beasts," he said, determination making his voice shake.

Elenna glanced at him. "Tom. Why—"

"Come on," he said, interrupting his friend. "We need to find the gloves. Let's eat. We won't find them while we're standing still."

Tom and Elenna travelled hard for the rest of the day, but when night fell they had no choice but to rest. As his friend slept beneath a rocky outcrop, Tom felt frustration burn in his heart. There had been no sign of the Beast, which meant that Tom was still no closer to completing his Quest.

Tom couldn't drift off. It was hard to ignore the constant throbbing of his injured hand and his mind was swirling with thoughts.

If I don't get to sleep soon, he thought, *I will be too tired to save Rokk*. He remembered a trick that his Uncle Henry had taught him, to help him sleep on restless nights.

"Look up at the stars and try to count them all," his uncle had said.

Tom unbuckled his sword and put it to one side. He lay back, staring up at the night sky. There were so many stars up there, it would take his whole life to count each one.

"One…two…three…four…" On and on. "Two-hundred-and-one, two-hundred-and-two…"

His eyelids began to feel heavy. Too heavy to keep open. A shooting star was the last thing that Tom saw, arcing across the night sky…

"Storm!" Elenna cried out, breaking into Tom's dream. His eyes snapped open and he scrambled to sit up. Storm was standing beside him.

He must have stood guard over me in the night, Tom realized. He was lucky to have such a faithful stallion. On the other side of the dead fire, Elenna was hastily gathering up their belongings.

"What's going on?" Tom croaked.

"A storm's coming!" Elenna replied, bundling blankets into Storm's saddlebags.

Tom leapt to his feet, all tiredness gone as he looked towards the valley. In the distance, trees swayed as a fierce wind – unnaturally fierce – tore its way across the land towards them.

"That's no normal storm," he said, feeling a tingle of fear in his stomach.

Elenna came to his side, shielding her eyes against the rising sun. "You're right, Tom," she said. "But I can't—" Elenna's words faded away as a writhing mass of black appeared on the horizon, streaming over the valley. It was heading straight for

them, moving faster than anything
Tom had ever seen.

"Bats," Tom whispered.

Scores of bats, moving fluidly like
a stream. Their wings flapped and
they screeched as they spread out,
suddenly above Tom and Elenna.
They circled the air, watching and
waiting. The gusts of wind created
by their wide leathery wings was
relentless, whipping Tom and
Elenna's hair and making their
eyes water. Storm and Silver stood
still, as if unsure which way to run.
Silver let out a howl of distress.

"Tom!" Elenna yelled, her voice
almost lost in the wind. "Their eyes!"

Tom craned his head and looked.
Each bat had a pair of eyes that
shone with a sickening shade of
blood-red. Tom felt his fists clench

with anger. He knew what this meant.

"Velmal has sent them!" he cried out. Elenna's face turned white with fear. Evil bats, that would stop at nothing, were about to attack them. How would they survive?

CHAPTER THREE

THE DARK WIZARD SPEAKS

Tom reached for the hilt of his sword, but his fingers closed around thin air.

"No!" he cried, glancing at the other side of the camp fire. There, glinting, Tom's weapon lay uselessly on the ground. "I don't have my sword!"

"I'll get it," Elenna said. "I'm closer." She scrambled over to where

Tom had been sleeping. Immediately, one of the bats broke from the circling formation and swooped down through the air to swipe a cruel claw at her face.

"Elenna!" Tom cried, warning his friend. "Look out!"

She threw both hands over her head, rolling forwards to grab Tom's sword. The bat landed on her arm, sinking its talons into her flesh.

Elenna screamed in agony and Tom saw thin streams of blood seeping from where the bat's claws had pierced her skin. He tried to run to her but the swarm of bats descended, screeching.

Their leathery wings slapped against Tom's body and their claws tangled in his hair. He dropped to his knees and fought the bats off.

"Get away!" he cried out. But it was impossible.

Glancing up, Tom saw Elenna struggling to shake off the bat that still clung to her bloodied limb. She dropped Tom's sword, which clattered to the ground, and kicked the hilt, sending the weapon skidding through the dirt. It came to a stop at Tom's feet.

Tom scooped it up with his right

hand; he almost dropped it again, crying out with pain. He glanced down at his hand and saw that the fingers were badly swollen, and had turned a darker shade of green. It was the poison coursing through his blood! *But Elenna needs me*, he thought desperately – he could not give in to the pain.

All of his friends needed him. Storm pawed the ground, tossing his head against the bats that were swarming around him. Silver growled as he leapt into the air and snapped his jaws. The bats' leathery wings skimmed the air above his head.

Clutching his sword in both hands, Tom swung it left and right, up and down. He didn't stop moving and felt his blade connect with thick, leathery wings and furry bodies. His muscles

began to scream with the effort of
keeping the weapon above his head,
but Tom wouldn't stop thrusting his
sword against the dark cloud of
enemies. Finally, the bat swarm
scattered, screeching in fear and rage.
Tom strode over to Elenna. A vivid
streak of blood ran down her elbow.

"Get it off me!" she cried, as the bat
still clung to her arm.

With a yell, Tom swung his sword. The bat screeched and released its grip on Elenna's arm. It joined the other bats and they flew away in a pulsating dark cloud, their angry cries filling the air. Finally silence descended and the bats were gone. But for how long?

Tom helped Elenna to her feet. Silver bounded over to his mistress, whining anxiously.

"There, there," Elenna said, patting her wolf's head. "No harm done." Tom wasn't so sure.

"My phoenix talon will heal those cuts," Tom said, inspecting Elenna's arm. The scratches ran deep.

"Later," Elenna told him, pointing up to the sky.

Tom looked up. The bats had already returned. They circled in the air, slow and menacing, silhouetted against the morning sun.

Tom raised his sword. "Come down and fight!" he shouted.

A low voice, full of evil mirth, sounded on the wind. Tom and Elenna looked at each other.

"Velmal," Elenna whispered faintly.

"Show yourself!" Tom cried.

The dark wizard laughed. "Do you really think I'd waste my energy in a swordfight with you? Besides, you will need more than a sword to overcome your next challenge."

"While there's blood in my veins," Tom shouted, "I'll succeed. And when I free the last Beast, I am coming for you!"

The wizard's laughter grew louder, as the swarm of bats arranged themselves into a long, thin line.

"I look forward to that day," said Velmal. "Until then…"

With an ear-piercing screech, the line of bats surged forward. Tom threw up his sword as he was struck by wings and claws. It was all he could do to stay on his feet. Then the bats swept through their camp and disappeared over the horizon.

The silence was heavy. Tom sheathed his sword, looking at Elenna, who was comforting Silver. "That's the last time I ever leave my sword out of reach," he vowed.

"We're all alive," said Elenna. "That's the main thing." Her voice tailed off. She was looking at something beyond Tom's shoulder.

"Oh, Tom," she whispered, raising a hand to point. Tom spun round on his heels.

"Storm!" he cried out, running to his stallion. The horse's legs were quivering, his flanks heaving as his eyes rolled back in his head.

"What's wrong with him?" Tom asked.

Elenna's face paled as she arrived at his side. "Oh no!"

"What is it?" said Tom. Elenna's fingers smoothed back Storm's coat at the side of his neck. There, Tom saw two puncture-wounds, about the same size as bat teeth. The wounds were new, and were a raw shade of red.

Tom felt anger flood his chest. "Storm's been bitten…"

CHAPTER FOUR

SAVING STORM

"Have the bites poisoned Storm?"
Tom cried. Elenna peered at the
wounds.

"There's no way of telling," she said.

Tom checked Storm's eyes. They
didn't seem glazed or dull. His legs
had stopped quivering and his
breathing was slowly calming down.
Silver paced around Storm, howling
mournfully.

"We'll know later," Elenna said. "If he continues to improve, we'll know it was just a normal bite. Vicious, but not actually poisonous. Let's hope he gets better."

Tom picked up his shield. He took out the phoenix talon that he had won from Epos the flame bird – oldest of Avantia's Good Beasts – and held it against Storm's injuries. The red, angry wounds pulsed for a moment, then shrank. It wasn't long before they had completely faded away.

"Hurry up and get better, boy," Tom whispered, patting Storm's flank.

"Aren't you forgetting someone?" a voice asked.

Tom turned to see Elenna holding out her injured arm, smiling.

Tom grinned back at her as he set the talon to work.

"Next time," he said, "if I stray too far from my sword, I'll be the one who goes to get it."

"Deal!" she said. "Then you can brave the bat claws!"

After packing up camp, they walked Storm along the path. They didn't want to ride him until he was completely better. The sky above them was almost obscured by high, sheer mountains. Ahead, Silver bounded swiftly, stopping every once in a while to sniff the air.

Tom checked the map on the amulet. "We're close to the gloves," he told Elenna. "But the path is sloping uphill again. This way."

Tom guided Storm to the left. Elenna whistled at Silver, who scampered over to them as they arrived at the foot of another sloping rocky road. This path was steeper and more treacherous. As they began to climb, Tom felt his leg muscles burn. Beside him, Elenna was breathing heavily.

"Is it me," she said, "or does it feel like there's no air up here?"

Tom nodded. "The air's getting thinner as we get higher," he said. "But don't worry. The plateau where the gloves are meant to be hidden is close. We can rest there."

Elenna bent down to pat Silver's head. The wolf's tongue lolled. He looked exhausted. "Not long, I promise," she said, her voice a quiet wheeze.

Tom stroked Storm's mane. He pulled his hand away and gasped; clumps of mane had stuck to his palm. Had Storm been poisoned after all? Tom turned to Elenna, showing her his hand. Her eyes widened.

"We'd better finish this Quest quickly," she said. "For Storm's sake."

Tom and Elenna strode up to the sheer rock-face, where the amulet had indicated the gloves were hidden. There was no choice: they would have to start climbing.

"I'll go first," Tom said. "If it's too treacherous, I want you to stay here."

"I'll be fine," Elenna said. "I won't let you go on alone." Tom was glad he had such a brave friend.

He slung his shield over his shoulder, then began climbing very carefully. Each hand and foothold was nothing more than a sliver of rock, barely enough to support him. As he moved, hand over hand, he heard Elenna following him.

Finally, Tom came upon a cranny wide enough to thrust his arm into. His stomach tingled with excitement; surely the gloves were here, it was a perfect hiding place! He plunged his arm into the crevice, all the way up to his shoulder. His fingers flexed as

he swept his hand left and right.
There was nothing but dust and
pebbles.

"Anything?" Elenna called.

Tom looked down at her. He could
see sweat forming on her brow, her
face red from the effort of climbing.

"No," he said. "But it can't be far."

He began climbing again. His arms and legs felt weaker now. His fingers trembled and he had to be much more careful with each movement, or he was going to fall. His arms felt as if they were on fire, his hair was soaked with sweat.

He heard a strange rattling sound from above, and his body froze. He looked up, almost losing his grip when a small chunk of rock bounced past him. He craned his neck back to look up at where the small rock had come from.

Descending the mountain was a tall, white-haired man in tatty grey robes.

Tom looked down at Elenna. "Go back," he hissed.

"Why?" Elenna asked, frowning.

Tom looked up at the approaching

man. His back was stooped and the expression on his face was fierce. They couldn't afford to be seen. Tom didn't want anyone trying to stop their Quest.

"Someone's coming!" he hissed.

CHAPTER FIVE

DEATH LEDGE

Tom and Elenna carefully climbed
back down to join their animal
companions. Elenna knocked loose
a chunk of rock and fell the last short
distance to the ground. Tom scrambled
down as she got to her feet.

"Are you hurt?" he asked.

"I'll survive," she replied, panting,
as she retrieved her bow and arrow.
"It wasn't a big fall." She looked back

at the mountain. "Was that Velmal again?"

Tom shook his head. "No. It's someone I've never seen before." As the man's face appeared over a lip of rock, peering down at them, Tom's hand went to the hilt of his sword, ready for whatever might happen. There was no hiding from the stranger now.

"I've never seen such an old man climb so high," Elenna whispered.

"Me neither," agreed Tom. His eyes didn't leave the man's face.

Together, they watched as he descended. When he hit the plateau, he turned. "Greetings, strangers!" he exclaimed. He was old, but up close he looked strong. He aimed a thick finger at them. "Who are you?"

Tom raised his hands in a peaceful

gesture. "We're travellers," he said. "Heading north."

The old man crossed his arms and frowned. His face was lined and craggy, like the mountains. "That's foolish," he said. "There's nothing there since the avalanche in Tion. Everyone's leaving in droves. Even me! The mountains have been my home my whole life, but they're no longer safe."

"I know nothing of Tion," Tom told him. "We're just…looking for something." Tom felt his heart beat faster. He knew that sounded very suspicious, but Aduro had taught him long ago it was usually safer not to tell anyone about his Beast Quests.

The old man cast his eyes about him. "There's nothing to find here," he said.

"Please," said Elenna. "If someone wanted to hide something here, where might they leave it?"

The man furrowed his wrinkled brow. "What do you seek?"

"Something important," Tom said, hoping there wouldn't be any more questions.

The stranger turned. "Over there," he said, pointing to a jagged outcrop of rock far above them. "What you're looking at," continued the old man, "is Death Ledge. If anything has been carefully hidden, it will be there. At night you can sometimes see a golden glow from Death Ledge. But you'd be foolhardy to climb it. One slip, one mistake, and you're dead."

"Thank you," Tom said, staring at the ledge. How was he ever going to reach that place?

"You want my advice?" said the old man, walking down the hill. "Turn back now."

Soon, he had disappeared down the mountain path.

Elenna pointed up at Death Ledge. "You can't climb that. It's impossible."

Tom took a deep breath. "Nothing's impossible," he replied, trying to convince himself as much as Elenna. "This time, I'll go alone. You stay with Silver and Storm. That's the best way you can help right now."

Elenna looked hesitant, then nodded. "Be careful," she said, as Tom approached the sheer rock face.

He began to climb, moving slowly and carefully. His arms ached, and he could barely grip anything with his right hand – but he had to find the gloves. Soon, Death Ledge cast a shadow to Tom's right, and he adjusted his climbing style so that he moved almost diagonally. Elenna and the animals were now so far below he couldn't see them. His arms started trembling – not from exhaustion, but from the sudden cold of the air this far from the ground.

Keep going, he told himself. *Hold on*. Now, he wasn't only climbing for the

Quest. He was climbing for his life.

As he got closer to Death Ledge, his stomach lurched; the outcrop leaned out over a terrifying drop. The view below was obscured by mist and clouds. Tom had no idea what waited for him down there and he couldn't afford to find out.

Just a bit further.

He got to an arm's length of the ledge, but the rock face was as smooth as ice – there was nothing for Tom to hold on to. If he wanted to reach Death Ledge, he would have to jump.

Tom held his breath and kicked off, throwing himself towards the outcrop. The thin wind howled in his ears, and his body felt completely weightless. For a moment, it was almost like flying.

"*Ooof!*" Tom gasped as his body slammed into the side of the ledge. His fingers desperately groped for a handhold as his legs dangled. Clenching his teeth, Tom heaved himself up, sweat running into his eyes. Finally, he was able to lift up a leg and roll to safety. He lay on his back, breathing heavily as he gazed at the bright blue sky. His relief made him laugh out loud.

Focus, he thought. *There's no time to waste*.

He sat up and began searching Death Ledge. He ran his fingertips over the mountain wall, moving loose stones in cracks and fissures.

"The gloves must be here," he muttered. "They're just very carefully hidden."

Drawing his sword, he worked the

tip into a crack, twisting the blade to loosen gravel and pebbles. Nothing. He moved on to another crevice and did the same. Again, nothing. But on his third attempt…

"Gold!" he exclaimed, as he gently drew his blade from a fissure. He could see a golden box buried deep within the gap. The box scraped against the sides of the opening, but finally Tom held the casket in his hands. Made of solid gold, the ornate box was small enough for Tom to hold in one hand, but almost as heavy as his sword.

Crack! Suddenly, Tom's body was thrown forwards and he had to

clutch the box to his chest. Another
loud cracking sound echoed through
the air.

"What's happening?" Tom cried. He
glanced down at his feet to see that
the rocky outcrop was now covered
with a web of jagged breaks. The
ground beneath his feet shuddered
and dipped.

Death Ledge was crumbling!

CHAPTER SIX

FALLING!

The rocky outcrop smashed like
shattered glass. Tom fell, still clutching
the box. His body spun and flipped in
mid-air. His legs and free arm flailed
as he tried to right himself. But it was
no good.

I'm falling to my death, Tom thought.
Faintly, he could hear Elenna crying
out far below.

He needed to unhook his shield.

69

Only Arcta's eagle feather would save
him now.

Tom twisted his body round so that
he was falling feet-first. Now he was
able to unhook his shield and hold it
above his head. Immediately, his
plummeting body slowed down,
swaying from side to side. He held
the golden box tight to his body as
he descended.

From his high vantage point, Tom saw a ruined, deserted town to the north of Gwildor. He knew that had to be Tion, the place the old man had mentioned. Homes and trees lay in tatters. There was not a single person to be seen.

He landed gently, near Elenna and his animal friends. Elenna ran over to him, followed by Silver. Storm stayed where he was, head lowered.

"Thank goodness you survived," Elenna said, sounding relieved.

"Of course I survived," he said. But he knew how lucky he'd been.

"Are the gloves in there?" she asked, eyes wide as she gazed at the golden box. Tom held up the casket.

"I think so," he said, feeling himself smile. "I haven't looked inside yet."

"Well, open it," said Elenna. "It's

beautiful. Whatever's inside must be good!"

Tom laughed in agreement. He ran his hands over the box, admiring the patterns etched into the precious metal. His fingertips brushed against something rough on the underside of the box. He turned it over. Etched on the bottom was an image of a suit of armour that Tom would have recognised anywhere – it was a copy of the Golden Armour that belonged to Avantia's Master of the Beasts. Beside it was an etching of another suit of armour – smaller, with spiked gauntlets and what looked like jewels embedded in the arms.

"I don't understand," said Elenna. "Why is a picture of your father's armour on a box in Gwildor?"

Tom thought hard, gazing at the

second set of armour. "All the prizes hidden in Gwildor belong to Freya," he muttered. "Perhaps the other set of armour belongs to her. The two sets of armour could symbolize Avantia's twinning with Gwildor?"

Tom turned the box over again. It was time to open it and find his next prize. The lid lifted with a loud creak, revealing a pair of gloves unlike any Tom had ever seen before.

Elenna bent closer. "They look so…fragile," she whispered.

She was right. The gloves were a dull silver, so thin they were almost transparent. It was as if they had been spun from the silk of spiders' webs. Tom was almost afraid to touch them.

As gently as he could, Tom lifted the gloves from the casket. Elenna

took the box from him and he
worked the fingers of his left hand
inside one of the gloves, shuddering
at the gentle touch of the cloth. He
put on the second glove. They were
light as air, but once Tom's hands
were inside, he felt strength flowing
through them. Even his injured hand
felt powerful.

He flexed his fingers, and then
bunched his hands into fists. But
when he tried to open them again,
his fingertips were stuck to his palms!

"These gloves...are...extra-sticky!"
Tom groaned. He had to use all his
strength to prise his hands open
again. He looked up at Elenna,
eyebrows raised in surprise and
amusement.

"That's going to create problems,"
said Elenna.

"Or solve them," Tom replied, realising what the gloves were for. "With these on, I can climb anything. If Rokk's home is the mountains, these gloves are going to help me get to him."

Elenna's eyes brightened. "That's amaz—"

Her voice was cut off by a dull thud. As they looked in the direction that the sound had come from, Elenna gasped. Tom felt his heart pounding.

Storm had collapsed.

CHAPTER SEVEN

AN INVISIBLE BEAST?

Tom and Elenna scrambled over to where the horse lay on the ground, his mighty legs collapsed beneath him. Close up, Tom could see that bald patches had appeared on Storm's coat. He could hear the stallion's weak, rasping breaths and smell the sweat coming off him as he shifted about uncomfortably.

Elenna pulled an eyelid back to inspect the whites of Storm's eyes. Tom could see how yellow they had become.

"Now we know," she said, her voice choked. "The bat's bite was poisonous after all."

"There must be something we can do!" Tom said.

Elenna shook her head, her eyes wide with helplessness. "If we could find a willow tree, I might be able to make some medicine from the bark. But I haven't seen a single willow tree in Gwildor."

Tom felt his stomach tighten. "Me neither," he said. "No, wait…I have." He closed his eyes. A picture of broken trees filled his mind. Where had he seen them? Of course – Tion!

"There are willow trees in Tion,"

he said. "I'm sure of it. I saw them when I was falling."

"I hope that Gwildor's medicines work the same as Avantia's," Elenna replied, scrambling to her feet.

"I'll go," Tom said, peeling off Freya's gloves. "You look after—"

With a loud whicker, Storm tossed his head and forced himself to his feet. Despite the poison coursing through his veins, the horse proudly raised his head.

"He's fighting the venom," Tom said, feeling a surge of pride in his chest. "He wants to carry on with us."

"I say we should listen to him," Elenna said. "Storm knows if he can carry on." She took hold of the reins, ready to walk with the stallion.

Tom placed the gloves in the

saddlebag. Then he gave Storm a pat as they set off. "Let's get to Tion quickly," he said to Elenna. "There we will find the cure for Storm...and the next Beast."

They walked as fast as they could, Silver scampering ahead, as usual. Storm eventually increased his pace to a trot, with Tom and Elenna running beside him; neither of them wanted to ride Storm in his weakened state. Tom wondered if the horse knew how ill he was, and was racing the poison.

"Oh no!" gasped Elenna, suddenly.

"What?" Tom asked.

"The golden casket," she said. "We left it behind."

"That's all right," Tom told her. "I've got the gloves. The casket belongs to Freya. One day, she'll find it, I'm sure."

Tom slipped out of the saddle and stood at the gateway to Tion. His gaze travelled over collapsed huts, remnants of thatched roofs, trees reduced to stumps. All around the empty town, mountains loomed. Only an avalanche could destroy a town in this way – but there were no rocks to be seen anywhere.

"Maybe it wasn't an avalanche," Tom said, thinking out loud. "Maybe a Beast came through here."

Elenna nodded. "That would explain why there are no people around."

"Come on," said Tom. "Let's find the willow trees. We can take Storm to one of the surviving huts and see if we can cure him."

Tom grabbed Storm's reins to walk him further into Tion. He felt the

familiar twinge of pain in his bad
hand. Tom led Storm to the nearest
house and the stallion obediently
ducked his head as he was led
through the front door. A half-eaten
breakfast of eggs and a full glass of
milk were still on the table in the far
corner. Opposite, there was a small,
unmade bed.

"These people left in a hurry,"
Elenna remarked, looking around.

As Tom settled Storm, a huge *bang*
sounded above them, startling the
stallion and causing Silver to bark
anxiously. Dust rained down on
Tom's shoulders and he glanced up
to see that the roof of the hut was
caving in. Straw fell like heavy rain.
Tom and Elenna scrambled back to
the walls, with Silver sheltering
behind Elenna's legs. With a weak

neigh, Storm managed to trot into a corner of the devastated hut.

Something long and brown reached down into the building: a huge stone arm! It had punched through the hut's roof!

Rokk.

"Let's get out of here!" Tom called, drawing his sword.

Elenna grabbed Silver by the scruff of the neck, while Tom ran over to Storm. The stallion was paralysed with terror. As he grabbed the reins, Tom heard a low, grating sound – it sounded almost like a roar – followed by a *whoosh*. Tom could picture the giant arm being drawn back to swing.

"WATCH OUT!" he called to Elenna.

Stone and straw went flying in all directions. The Beast had ripped the rest of the roof clean off the hut.

Tom ducked, throwing his arms over his head. Dust and mortar showered down. Tom couldn't see, and could barely breathe. His eyes, ears and nose were clogged with dust. Splintered wood and shattered rock ricocheted off his body, grazing his skin. Tom ran a hand over his shoulder and felt a bruise already swelling. *Pain will have to wait*, he thought. *I have a Quest to complete.*

Everything became still. Tom straightened up, dust falling off him, and looked about. Elenna was safe but formed a ghostly silhouette, covered in dust.

"What was that?" she asked.

Tom felt sick with nerves as he drew his sword. "Rokk," he said, pulling his shield from his back. "It had to be."

Elenna came to stand beside him. "But…where is he?"

Tom looked about. Where the walls of the hut had once stood, there was now a perfect view over the mountains. But there was no sign of the Beast. As fast as he'd arrived, he'd gone again.

Tom lowered his sword, frowning.

"I don't understand it," he said. "Rokk's disappeared."

CHAPTER EIGHT

INTO BATTLE

"How can a Beast just disappear?" Elenna asked, staggering out of the broken hut.

"Maybe it's one of Rokk's special powers," Tom mused. "Invisibility?"

Elenna shook her head and smiled grimly. "Well, that's just not fair, is it?"

Behind them, Storm gave a weak snort. Tom and Elenna turned to look at the stallion. Silver stood beside him, covered in dust. The wolf shook his fur, but Storm stood perfectly still, not caring about the dust that clogged his patchy coat.

"Storm's losing the fight," Elenna said. "We need the willow bark now!"

Tom felt a surge of anger. How could he save Storm *and* defeat Rokk, who could spring a surprise attack at any moment? "Curse you, Velmal!" he yelled, shaking a fist at the sky.

"Don't worry, Tom," said Elenna, pointing to a cluster of willow trees a short distance away. "Look!"

Elenna sprinted over to the trees, drawing her hunting knife mid-stride. Tom guarded Storm and Silver, sword and shield at the ready, eyes alert for any sign of the Beast. He felt a prickle of fear crawl up his spine.

I might not be able to see Rokk, he

realized. *But that doesn't mean the Beast isn't watching me.*

He was dimly aware of Elenna reaching across a broken willow tree when the air rumbled with that same low, grating sound they had heard before. Rokk was nearby. But where?

"Come out," Tom whispered, with his back to Elenna. "Show yourself."

"TOM!"

Elenna's scream had him spinning round on his heels. Storm snorted and Silver yelped in fear. The face of the nearest mountain seemed to be writhing, surging forwards like a giant tidal wave, carrying Elenna with it.

The hidden Beast was revealing himself! Rocks and rubble were blasted into the air, fusing together to form…a giant! The huge stone Beast strode forwards on long, stony legs. His thick arms were knotted with muscles the size of boulders – they *were* boulders!

Elenna was clinging to one of the arms, her face pale. Rokk tried to shake her off, but Elenna hung on. Her feet kicked and her screams of fear echoed though the air.

Tom darted forwards, ready to hack his blade at the Beast's shins. Rokk stamped a foot, sending a tremor rippling through the ground, which was powerful enough for Tom to lose his footing. He had to stab his sword into the ground to stop himself from sprawling in the dirt.

With a flick of his mighty arm, Rokk flung Elenna aside. Tom watched her body twist in the air as she moved in a wide, slow arc.

"ELENNA!" Tom cried, as his friend crashed through a thatched roof. He jumped to his feet and started running over to her, dimly aware of Silver racing behind him.

Tom reached the hut. Elenna lay on her back, unmoving. Tom could see a bruise on her left cheek and cuts on her neck and arms – but she was breathing. She was alive! Silver nosed his mistress, trying to wake her up.

"You look after her for me," Tom told the wolf. "I have a Quest to complete…" He'd have to heal her cuts and bruises after he'd liberated the Beast.

Tom turned and marched out of the broken hut. He hated to leave Elenna, but if he didn't face up to Rokk, an entire kingdom would be ruined.

Storm was leaning against the side of the building, shallow breaths making his body shudder as sweat streaked down his coat.

I'm sorry, my friend, Tom thought. *Hold on*.

He turned to face the Beast.

Rokk towered over the ruined village of Tion. Tom looked up into the face of the Beast, noticing that one of his eyes was shining green. By now, Tom recognised the mark of Velmal's poison, which kept the Beast under his dark spell. Green dust fell from Rokk's shoulders.

"It's you and me, now," Tom said to the Beast. "One-on-one." He didn't care if Rokk understood or not.

The huge Beast smashed his fists together, the sound of their collision as loud as an avalanche.

"You don't frighten me," Tom said, aiming the point of his blade at the Beast. "This is for my friend!"

He charged.

Tom saw his opponent draw back both stony arms, preparing to strike. With a battle cry that tore at his throat, Tom rolled forwards to duck under the deadly arms, hearing the rumble as Rokk's fists punched the ground. He jumped up and swung his

sword as hard as he could, right to left. He didn't even have time to feel the pain in his injured hand, but his sword clanged uselessly off Rokk's limbs.

Rokk rose up to his full height. His boulder-head glanced down at Tom, whose gaze was drawn to Rokk's right eye – the one that shone green. "That's where I need to get to," he murmured.

If he could somehow remove the source of the green light, Tom was sure he could free the Beast. To do that, he'd have to climb all the way to the Beast's head. But how could he do that? The answer came to Tom in a thunderbolt.

"The magic gloves!" he cried.

CHAPTER NINE

A NASTY SURPRISE

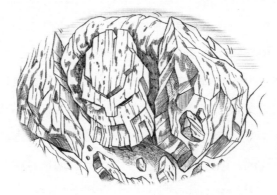

Tom ran into the hut and pulled the
gloves from Storm's saddlebag. But as
he raced back outside, Rokk was
throwing punch after mighty punch,
destroying buildings as he strode
towards Tom. Leaning down, the
Beast threw another punch. Tom
ducked out of the way just in time
and felt dust and pebbles clatter
down on his shoulders from the

Beast's huge body.

The Beast wasn't going to give up. He kicked out and lunged, letting out roars of anger that rattled and echoed in his throat. Tom jumped and ducked, rolled and weaved to avoid being crushed by the fists of stone. He tried to leap onto the Beast's leg, but Rokk was too strong, flicking him off like a fly. Tom landed heavily on the dusty ground, winded and frustrated.

Rokk lifted his left arm and brought his fist crashing down towards Tom.

"No!" Tom cried, leaping out of the way. He lunged with his sword towards a moss-filled groove in the Beast's rock-solid leg, but Rokk threw out his arm and with a roar of anger sent Tom spinning away.

Tom clambered to his feet, holding his sword out in front of him. The blade shook unsteadily in the air, as Tom's injured hand struggled to maintain its grip. A moment of doubt flooded his mind.

Can I do this? he wondered. He needed a new tactic to suceed.

Lowering his sword, he noticed fragments of moss clinging to its blade. It was moss from the joints in Rokk's leg, where Tom had struck a moment ago. Was this moss linking Rokk's body together, like glue? Was it the only thing keeping him standing up? And if Tom cut away the moss, could he destroy the rock Beast?

"It's worth a try," Tom muttered. But he needed all the help he could get.

The purple jewel! he thought, remembering the prize he had gathered for defeating Sting, the scorpion-man. The jewel endowed his sword with the power to break rock.

Tom gripped his sword tighter, willing himself to ignore the twinges of pain in his right hand. He advanced, staying just out of the Beast's reach. "Come on," he called. "Try and get me!"

The Beast raised his left leg and brought it smashing down. As he jumped aside, Tom heard the earth rattle from the impact. But now Tom was beside a moss-filled groove in Rokk's leg. He plunged his sword deep into it, calling on the power of the purple jewel. He heard the stone crack and splinter, and clumps of moss flew away. Tom's blade ground against the rock, sending out sparks that showered his face. Rokk roared with pain, raising his chest towards the sky and bunching his fists. Rokk's upper body dipped and lurched. He flung out his arms.

"Keep going," Tom told himself. "Don't stop now." He thrust his sword again and again, aiming the point of his blade towards any moss-filled crevice. Soon moss littered the ground at his feet and Rokk was too stunned from the pain to fight back. He was swaying in the air above Tom's head, trying to keep his balance. Tom paused, wiping the sweat from his brow as he gazed up at the mighty Beast. Rokk tipped to the left, at the mercy of his broken body. Then, with a stony roar of despair, the Beast toppled like a chopped tree, arms flailing.

When he hit the ground, Rokk's body shattered. Rocks and boulders

flew in every direction and Tom had
to leap out of the way behind one of
the last buildings left standing.

All was silent.

Tom's heart dropped. He hadn't
meant to destroy the Beast in this
way. He had wanted to slow Rokk
down long enough to climb up to his
face and remove the object of Velmal's
enchantment.

"I'm sorry," Tom muttered as he
stepped out and surveyed the rubble.
He turned to walk back to the hut
where Elenna was, when...

Clack!

Crunch!

Thunk!

Tom spun round. The hair on the
back of his neck stood up. The
remains of the Beast were sliding
along the dusty ground and fusing

back together. Rokk was reforming!
With an angry roar, he dug his fists
into the earth as he heaved himself
up to his feet. Soon, he was standing
as tall as ever, with every limb intact.
His two hollow eyes narrowed with
fury.

*How do I defeat a Beast who can heal
himself so quicky?* Tom thought.

With his gloves!

He reached into his pocket to pull them out, sliding his hands inside their feather-light folds. It was time to climb.

Tom ran towards Rokk as fast as he could. He launched himself forwards, hands outstretched. The walking mountain swung his left leg in a fierce, deadly kick. Tom's hands latched onto his shin, his grip perfect, as he climbed up the Beast's limb. His hands were stuck so tight to the rock that with each move it took all of Tom's strength to release his grip. Slowly and carefully, he made his way up to Rokk's waist. The Beast twisted round, trying to knock Tom off his body, but he wasn't flexible enough to reach him. For now, Tom was safe.

I can't believe I'm climbing a Beast, Tom thought. He made his way up and round to the great expanse of Rokk's chest. This was even more dangerous than climbing to Death Ledge.

His heart pounded hard when he heard a scraping sound. Looking up, he saw that Rokk had pulled back both arms and Tom knew that they were coming down to crush him. He had to time this just right...

As the deadly stone limbs came plunging down with a low *whoosh*, Tom kicked off. Rokk missed Tom, hitting himself in the torso so hard that his body buckled.

Tom threw his arms up, his hands latching on to the Beast's head.

He was hanging onto Rokk's eye socket.

CHAPTER TEN

THE FINAL BATTLE

Tom heaved himself up and rolled inside the eye socket, shielding his eyes from the bright green light that filled the gaping chasm.

Tom turned and peered out of the giant's eye. He saw the Beast's rocky hands scrabble desperately at his face. Tom scrambled further inside the socket, out of reach. If he didn't conquer Velmal's magic soon, who knew what damage Rokk would do to himself?

What's creating the green light? Tom thought. He glanced around. There! A piece of jade the size of an orange was set deep into the cavernous eye-socket.

"I'll have to be quick," Tom gasped, running towards the jade. But suddenly he was slammed against the sides of the hollow socket. Almost immediately, he found his body thrown against the other side and he cried out as his ribs rammed against stone.

Rokk was shaking his head!

He's trying to throw me out, Tom thought. He thrust out his hands, feeling the gloves latch onto the side of the socket. Rokk was swinging his head even more violently. Tom's

feet were lifted into the air as the
force of the movements shook the
bones in his body. Without the
gloves, Tom knew he would now
be falling.

For a moment, the shaking stopped
and Tom heard Rokk give a low
groan of pain. Tom heaved himself
up, feeling beads of sweat trickle
down his neck. He began to make his

way towards the jade, hands first. He didn't want any sudden movements to send him flying. Slowly and surely, he put one hand in front of the other, crawling across the floor of the eye socket. Each time he moved his hands, the gloves made a sticky, ripping sound. Tom was getting closer to the lump of jade, and had to duck his head against the glare.

Finally, the jade was in reach.

Tom closed his eyes against the ferocious green light. He extended his right arm until his fingers found the smooth, cool surface of the jade. He tugged, but it didn't move. Tom slapped his left hand onto the large stone, but it still refused to budge.

As Tom felt Rokk's head duck and thrash again, he gripped the jade with all his strength. Even his sticky gloves couldn't shift it. He'd need to use every last ounce of his strength. Leaping into the air, he planted his feet on the base of the semi-precious stone and heaved.

"One…two…" Tom took a deep breath. "THREE!"

With a *crack* that cannoned off the walls, the lump of jade came free. The green light faded…but Tom's final, desperate heave sent him plummeting straight out of the Beast's eye!

My shield! he thought. As he fell, he tore one hand free of the jade and desperately scrabbled to unhook the shield.

"*Ooof!*" Tom gasped as he landed. The air flew out of his lungs and red spots of dizziness danced before his eyes. But he had not hit the ground; that was still a long way below.

He had landed in the centre of Rokk's outstretched palm!

Tom scrambled to his feet. If Rokk closed his hand, Tom would be crushed.

The Beast gazed at him, and an understanding seemed to pass between them.

He's good again, Tom realized.

Rokk's face split into a grin. Then he bent down and gently set Tom on the ground. Tom watched as Rokk's

head dipped once. A nod of thanks!
Then the Beast extended a hand,
palm open.

He wants the jade.

Tom placed the green stone in
Rokk's palm, shaking it free of his
sticky gloves. One by one, Rokk's
fingers closed around the jade,
crushing it. With a flick of his mighty
hand, Rokk sent the remains – thick,
green dust – into the air, where it
sprinkled over the town. Tom felt
his chest swell with delight. Another
Quest had been completed and
another Beast was free. The source
of Velmal's evil magic had been
destroyed.

"What did I miss?" asked a voice.

Tom turned to see Elenna limping
towards him.

"Elenna!" Tom cried. "You're all

right." She nodded, grinning. His friend was flanked by Silver and Storm. The stallion gave a neigh of greeting. His coat was glossy again and the dull glaze had melted from his eyes. He was healthy!

"You didn't miss much," Tom joked as they arrived at his side. "I just saved another Beast."

"So nothing big, then," Elenna replied, teasing him.

The two of them turned to watch Rokk walk back to the mountain from which he'd emerged. The Beast came to a halt before the mountain face. Slowly, the rocks that made up his body began to roll away and collect at the base of the mountain, until there was nothing left to see. Tom knew that the mighty Beast had returned to his home.

"Hopefully," Tom said, removing his magic gloves, "the people will now return and rebuild this town. Velmal's evil rein in Tion is over."

In no time at all, Tom had used his phoenix talon to heal Elenna's cuts and grazes. Then she scrambled up the slope to gather willow bark, which she steeped in water for Storm to drink.

"He's much better," she said happily. "But this medicine will help him heal even more quickly."

Though the stallion's coat was still bare in places, he was soon moving about with all his usual grace and energy.

"It might be a good idea to take some bark with us," Elenna said.

"You never know when it might come in useful."

"I'll get it," said Tom, jogging over to the cluster of trees by Rokk's mountain. He climbed a tree easily, even without the gloves, and was just unsheathing his sword when he glimpsed something out of the corner of his eye.

It can't be, he thought.

In the distance stood Freya, her eyes were locked on his. Tom found he couldn't look away.

The Mistress of the Beasts suddenly drew back a hand and hurled a jagged rock at Tom. He raised his shield, feeling the missile thunk against it and almost knock him out of the tree. With a scowl, Freya turned and disappeared over the mountain.

"Why would she...?" he began to

mutter. Then he looked to where the rock had landed. He scrambled down the tree, just as Elenna came running over.

"Where did that rock come from?" she asked.

"Freya," he answered.

Elenna gasped. "She's trying to kill you!"

Tom started to nod, but stopped as he peered closely at Freya's missile. It was so heavy, it had made a groove in the earth, uncovering buried twigs, leaves...and something dark and leathery.

"What's this?" Tom mused, kicking the rock away. He bent down and picked up a small leather bag with a strong strap.

Elenna frowned. "Who would bury that here?"

"I don't know," said Tom. "But it'll come in handy. I can put the prizes in here, so we don't overload Storm's saddlebags."

"Huh," said Elenna, her face breaking into a grin. "Bet Freya didn't expect that to happen when she threw the rock."

Tom felt tingles of excitement all over his body. "What if she did?" he asked. "What if the good part of her wanted to show me this? We can still save her, Elenna. I know we can!"

Elenna nodded. "Maybe," she said. "For now, we have a healthy horse again and a Quest to complete."

Tom took his magic gloves from his pocket and placed them in the new bag along with the magic pearl and ring that he had already won. Then he and Elenna walked over to Storm and Silver. Tom's body was totally exhausted, but he was full of energy and determination. While there was blood in his veins, he wouldn't give up – not on the Beasts, and not on the Beast Mistress.

"Let's get going," he said to Elenna, as he climbed into Storm's saddle. He gazed out over the mountains of Gwildor and felt the spirit of Rokk wishing him well. What new Beasts were waiting for him out there? He turned Storm towards the path and Elenna walked alongside, with Silver bounding ahead. Tom knew that all of them were ready to take on the fourth Beast.

"We'll do whatever it takes," Tom said.

Here's a sneak preview of Tom's
next exciting adventure!

Meet

KOLDO
THE ARCTIC
WARRIOR

Only Tom can free the Beasts from
Velmal's wicked enchantment...

PROLOGUE

Linus gasped when he saw the giant footprint in the snowdrifts. The stories were true.

"It's this way!" said Dylar, pointing a bony finger along the icy path ahead.

Flames licked the air from the torch in his other hand, and grey smoke curled up into the freezing night sky. Dylar was the village elder, and the orange light showed every wrinkle on his stern face.

Linus was only a child, but he carried a torch like everyone else. Despite the heat from the flames, he shivered inside his thick fur clothes. His village, Freeshor, was covered in snow all year round, but tonight the cold got into his bones like never before.

They were hunting a monster.

"There! There!" shouted someone. "I saw something!"

Shouts went up among the people of the village.

"Where?"

"After the beast!"

"There's no time to waste."

The crowd surged forward, but Dylar shouted louder than the rest: "Stop! Stay close together. We can't tackle this creature unless we work as a team. Send the young ones out of harm's way."

Linus made sure he wasn't among the children pushed to the rear. He slipped under hands and legs to stay near the front.

There's no way I'm going to miss the fun! he thought.

As the path dipped and narrowed, something glinted ahead.

"It's the Ice Monster!" a man cried. Linus held his breath.

The creature was facing away from them, thickset and as tall as two men. Its frozen body shone pale blue in the reflected torchlight. In some places, Linus could see right through its torso.

The Beast turned to them, and bellowed in anger. His face was made of flat surfaces and angles, like a half-finished statue. Icicles hung from his chin and brows, and his eyes were like frozen pools. Linus saw that the Beast was carrying a shield, almost as tall as Linus himself. It glowed a sickly green. In his other fist he clutched a jagged ice-club.

"Wh...what should we do?" someone asked.

With a creaking sound, the Ice Monster raised one foot, then brought it down hard on the ground. The path shook, and the villagers stumbled backwards. But the creature didn't come towards them.

"Surround him!" Dylar cried.

**Follow this Quest to the end in
KOLDO THE ARCTIC WARRIOR.**

Win an exclusive
Beast Quest T-shirt and goody bag!

Tom has battled many fearsome Beasts and we want to know
which one is your favourite! Send us a drawing or painting of
your favourite Beast and tell us in 30 words why you think
it's the best.

Each month we will select **three** winners to receive
a Beast Quest T-shirt and goody bag!

Send your entry on a postcard to
BEAST QUEST COMPETITION
Orchard Books, 338 Euston Road, London NW1 3BH.

Australian readers should email:
childrens.books@hachette.com.au

New Zealand readers should write to:
Beast Quest Competition, 4 Whetu Place, Mairangi Bay,
Auckland NZ, or email: childrensbooks@hachette.co.nz

**Don't forget to include your name and address.
Only one entry per child.**

Good luck!

Join the Quest,
Join the Tribe

www.beastquest.co.uk

Have you checked out the Beast Quest website?
It's the place to go for games, downloads, activities,
sneak previews and lots of fun!

You can read all about your favourite Beasts, down-
load free screensavers and desktop wallpapers for
your computer, and even challenge your friends
to a Beast Tournament.

Sign up to the newsletter at www.beastquest.co.uk
to receive exclusive extra content and the oppor-
tunity to enter special members-only competitions.
We'll send you up-to-date info on all the Beast
Quest books, including the next exciting series
which features six brand-new Beasts!

Get 30% off all Beast Quest Books at www.beastquest.co.uk
Enter the code BEAST at the checkout.

Series 5

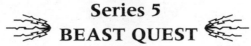

BEAST QUEST

Tom must travel to Gwildor, Avantia's twin kingdom,
to free six new Beasts from an evil enchantment...

978 1 40830 437 2

978 1 40830 438 9

978 1 40830 439 6

978 1 40830 440 2

978 1 40830 441 9

978 1 40830 442 6

SPECIAL BUMPER EDITION!

978 1 40830 436 5

Can Tom rescue the
precious Cup of Life
from a deadly
two-headed demon?

Series 6: WORLD OF CHAOS
Out now!

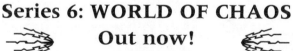

KOMODO
THE LIZARD KING

978 1 40830 723 6

MURO
THE RAT MONSTER

978 1 40830 724 3

FANG

978 1 40830 725 0

MURK
THE SWAMP MAN

978 1 40830 726 7

TERRA
CURSE OF THE FOREST

978 1 40830 727 4

VESPICK
THE WASP QUEEN

978 1 40830 728 1

SPECIAL BUMPER EDITION!

CRETA
THE WINGED TERROR

978 1 40830 735 9

Does Tom have the strength
to defeat terrifying Creta?

All books priced at £4.99.
Special bumper editions priced at £5.99.

Orchard Books are available from all good bookshops, or can
be ordered from our website: www.orchardbooks.co.uk,
or telephone 01235 827702, or fax 01235 8227703.